For Mum and Dad and Simon

With thanks to Paddington Pooka
for her example and assistance

This edition is
published and distributed
exclusively by
DISCOVERY TOYS
Martinez, CA

First published
in 1988 by
Walker Books, Ltd.
London

Printed in Italy

ISBN 0-939979-21-7

Wake Up Mr. B!

Penny Dale

DISCOVERY TOYS

Rosie woke up very early.

She went to wake up Billy.

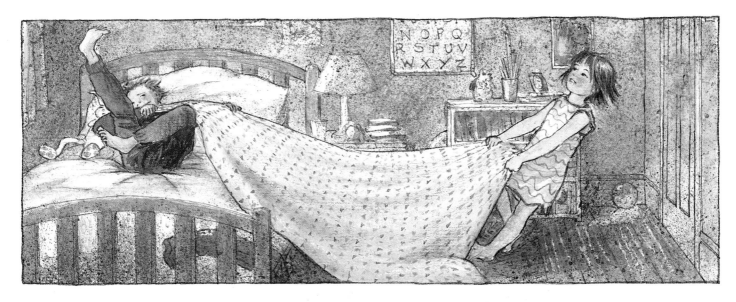

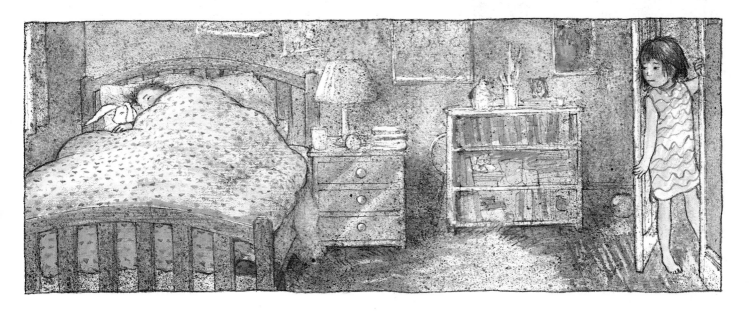

She went to wake up Dad.

She went to find Mr. B.

"Wake up, Mr. B," she said.

"Come with me, Mr. B," she said.

"Let's get dressed."

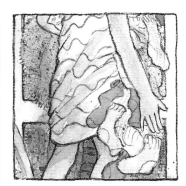

"Get in my car, Mr. B," she said.

"We're driving to the sea."

"Get in my boat, Mr. B," she said.

"We're sailing around the world."

"Get in my balloon, Mr. B," she said.

"Don't fall asleep. We're flying to the moon."

"Come and see Rosie and Mr. B," said Billy.

"Wake up, Rosie! Wake up, Mr. B!"